All About Danny

written and photographed
by
Mia Coulton

Here is my house.

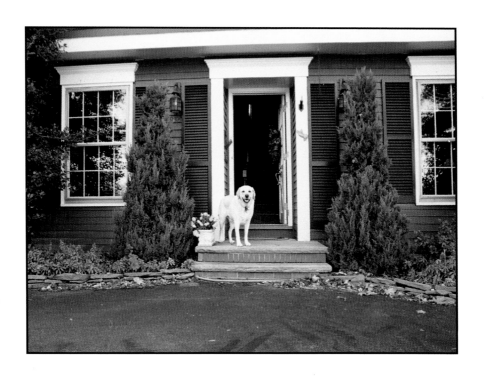

Here is my bed.

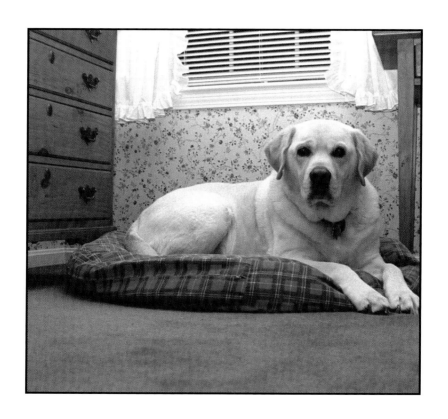

Here is my food.

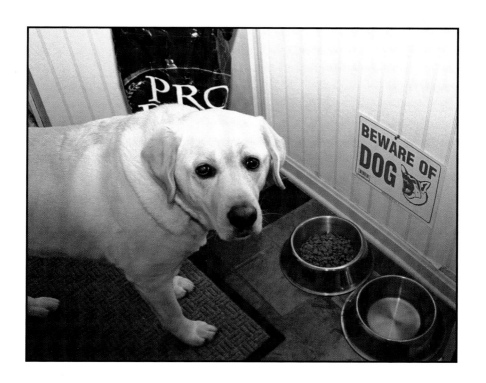

Here is my window.

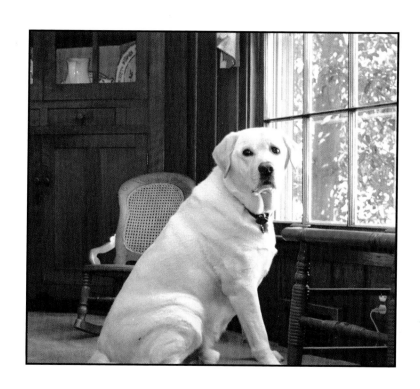

Here is my toy.

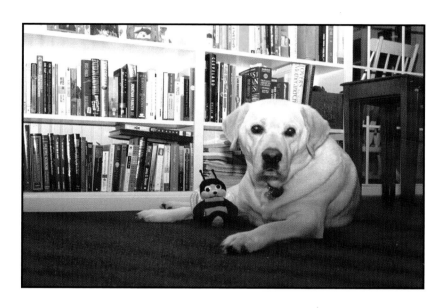

Bee

Here is my yard.

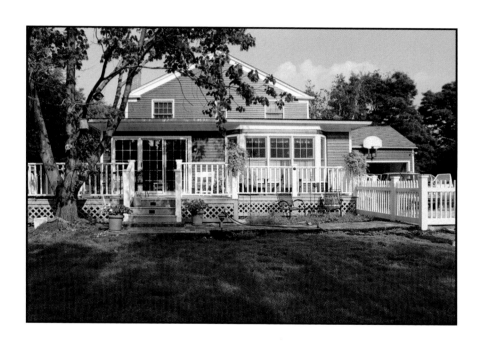

Here is my friend.

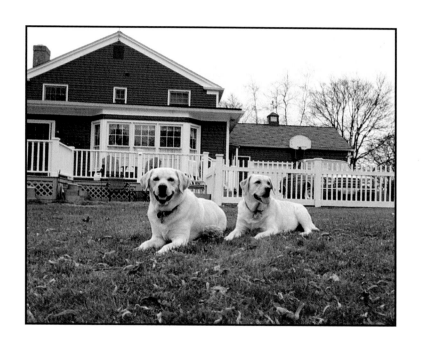

Abby

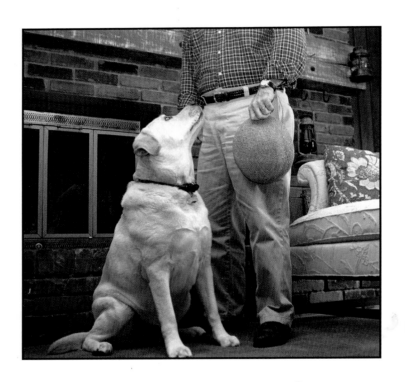

Here is Dad.